Keep me clean!

Please don't
handle me
with soiled hands.

Pierre

Story by

Mary Holman

Illustrated by

Sergio Ramirez

Villa Press
P.O. Box 33011
San Diego, California 92163-2011
International Standard Book Number 0-9641430-1-1
LIBRARY OF CONGRESS CATALOG CARD NUMBER 94-60875
Printed in Hong Kong

For all my nieces
and
nephews

Nikki (that's short for Nicole) had one brother and one baby sister — but still something was missing. One day she said to her father, "Dad, I'm lonely; I need a dog." But her father said, "I'm sorry, Nikki, but you can't have a dog. You're much too allergic to dogs."

Not only was Nikki allergic to dogs; she was also allergic to cats.

Whenever she would pet a dog or a cat she would sneeze and wheeze, and her eyes would puff red. Because of her sneezing, Nikki's father would never let her have a dog.

Poor Nikki walked around the neighborhood whistling at all the frisky puppies and fuzzy kittens.

She talked to them from the sidewalk as they barked
or purred in their yards. Nikki loved dogs and cats,
and they loved her too.

Nikki couldn't understand why her dad wouldn't let her have a dog.

 Why can't I have a dog? Colds make me sneeze; not dogs." Her father laughed. "Dad, I really need a dog." Nikki's dad stopped laughing and sternly informed Nikki that that was enough. Nikki still hoped for a dog. At night she knelt beside her bed and said a prayer for a pet dog. She knew her parents would not allow it, but she hoped somehow they would change their minds.

On the day before her birthday Nikki asked her mother, "Are you going to give me a dog for my birthday? I sure want a dog."

Her mother smiled and said, "No, Nikki, but you
will have a lovely surprise."

The next day her parents brought home a large green bird. "Happy birthday, Nikki." Nikki screamed, "Oh great, a parrot! Can he talk?"

She carried her new pet in his cage upstairs to her bedroom. "How nice to have a pet I can talk to," she thought.

Nikki set the parrot on her dresser and smiled. She whistled; the parrot whistled back. Next she said "Hello," but the parrot just sat.

S he said "Hello" again, and this time the parrot said, "*Bonjour* — hello." Nikki giggled with delight. "Since you speak French I'll call you Pierre." Nikki jumped with joy, but Pierre just sat. She ran around the cage, but Pierre just sat. She reached into the cage to hug Pierre, but he just flapped his wings.

What am I going to do with a bird who doesn't do anything but speak French?" Nikki asked herself. She couldn't think of a single thing.

She was so disappointed that she put Pierre in the back of her closet between the bride doll she had grown tired of and the roller skates which were too small. She closed the closet door and got ready for bed.

That night as she put her head on her pillow, she thought how nice it would be if Pierre were a dog, instead of a parrot.

She thought and thought until she fell into a fitful sleep. The hours went by as she tossed and turned and the clock on her bedstand ticked and ticked.

Suddenly the closet door swung open, and Pierre flew out and landed on Nikki's bed.

He nuzzled Nikki's cheek, and she opened her eyes. "What are . . . how did you . . .," Nikki tried to ask, but before she could finish Pierre cried, "*Allons à Paris* — let's go to Paris! *Prends-moi par la queue* — grab onto my tail." Still half-asleep Nikki held onto Pierre's tail, and out the window they flew.

Soon Nikki stood on a dark narrow street in Paris with Pierre on her shoulder.

Paris is, of course, the most important city in
France. They could smell bread baking, and they
soon discovered a bakery at the end of the street.
Wasting no time, they entered.

Bonjour," said a tall man with a white apron and a white hat. He had a long moustache and a friendly smile. Pierre said *"Bonjour,"* and Nikki also said *"Bonjour."* After all, that was all the French Nikki knew how to say. She wanted to order a loaf of bread, but she didn't know how to say it in French.

$\mathbb{P}$ierre sensed she was hungry. "*Une baguette, s'il vous plaît* — a loaf of bread, please," he said to the baker, and the baker handed Nikki a long, skinny loaf of bread. Nikki took a great big bite, and, after chewing completely and swallowing, she said to Pierre, "This bread tastes good. It's so fresh and soft to chew." Then she gave Pierre a taste. She said, "Pierre, do you like this French bread?" Pierre nodded and said, "*Mais oui* — of course."

After finishing half their bread, Nikki and Pierre wandered along the Champs Elysées, the main street in Paris.

Out of a bank ran a policeman chasing two bank
robbers. Nikki pointed to the robbers, and Pierre flew
into action. He flew over to one of the men and
grabbed him by the ear with his beak. Nikki ran close
behind and tripped the other robber with the remain-
ing bread.

The policeman handcuffed the two men.

As he led them away, everyone in the street shouted
"*Bravo*" to the heroes and hissed at the robbers.

$\mathbb{P}$ierre wanted to show Nikki the Army Museum, a
museum of soldiers. They rode the Metro, which is
the Paris subway, to the station nearest the museum.

From there they walked to the museum.

 Along the long halls were suits of armor that knights had worn. Nikki took down a sword from the wall. "Wow, Pierre, look at this!" A deep voice cried, *"En garde."* Nikki spun around to see a large knight waving a sword at her. Nikki screamed. "Pierre, this suit of armor has come to life!"

She held her sword in front of her, pointing it at the huge knight. The knight came closer, and Nikki shook with fear as she looked into his cold face. Pierre knew he needed to act quickly. He darted behind the knight. *"Derrière vous, Monsieur*—behind you, sir."* The knight turned toward Pierre, and Nikki then thrust her sword straight at the knight. The knight ran, his armor clanking, all the way to the end of the museum. Pierre cried, *"On a gagné*—we won!"*

Nikki was hungry from their battle with the knight so she looked for a McDonald's. Not far away she found one.

$\mathbb{P}$ierre ordered for Nikki, "*Un hamburger, des frites et un coca* — a hamburger, french fries and a Coke." Nikki took her meal and shared with Pierre who said to Nikki, "*J'aime les frites ici* — I like the french fries here. *Aimes-tu ces frites* — do you like these french fries?" Nikki smiled, but she was too busy chewing to answer.

After their meal they went to the Luxembourg Gardens.

Many people sat in this park looking at the pond and its big fountain. Nikki ran past them to the monkey bars and the slide. Pierre watched as she played. It had rained the day before so that Nikki was soon covered with mud. She had it on her shoes, on the seat of her pants, and even in her eyes. Nikki's eyes were stuck closed, and she fell fast asleep at the bottom of the slide.

Breakfast is ready." Nikki opened her eyes. She looked at the foot of her bed and saw her muddy shoes. She heard rain against the window. She jumped out of bed, opened the closet door and took Pierre in his cage out of the closet. She put him back on the dresser.

Nikki no longer wanted a dog. "What could be better than a parrot who speaks French?" she thought. Nikki smiled at Pierre. "Good morning, Pierre." "Bonjour," answered Pierre. "*Tu as aimé Paris* — did you like Paris?" Nikki answered, "Yes, Pierre, I loved it; can we go back soon?" "*D'accord, mon amie* — O.K., friend."

The End

La Fin

How Does the Word Sound?

ENGLISH	FRENCH	PRONUNCIATION
Hello	Bonjour	[bō(n)zhoor]
Let's go	Allons	[ahlō(n)]
Paris	Paris	[pahree]
Me	Moi	[mwah]
The tail	La queu	[lahkeuh]
Please	S'il vous plaît	[seelvooplay]
Yes	Oui	[wee]
Sir	Monsieur	[msyeuh]
French fries	Les frites	[layfreet]
O.K.	D'accord	[dahkōr]
My friend	Mon ami(e)	[mōnahmee]
The end	La fin	[lahfay(n)]

MYRTLE PHILIP SCHOOL